How to W
Edgar Al

by

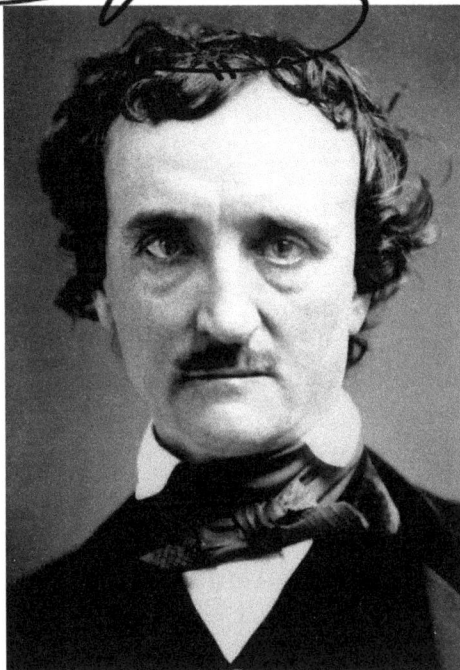

JBJ Books

How to Write like Edgar Allan Poe

Printed in the USA for

JBJ Books
From the Classics to the Cutting Edge™
www.jbjbooks.co.uk

Visit our site for our every growing catalogue of Classic and cutting edge titles available in a variety of media options.

Literature / Instruction / Poetry

Also available from JBJ books
How to Write like Alan Moore by Alan Moore
Edgar Allan Poe – The Collected Works

Introduction

Who better to teach the art of gothic horror story-telling, or heart stopping poetry than the master of the macabre and fantastic – Edgar Allan Poe himself?

Many books have been written by those trying to impart Poe's artistic technique for poems and short stories – both of which Poe considered to be the pinnacle of the story telling art but all fall short of coming close to allowing readers to really get 'into the skin' of the great man himself.

However readers will be thrilled to know that there is no need for second hand tutorials on how to write like Poe as the great man penned his several essays – everyone included here in their entirety – that did just that.

The Philosophy of Composition was published posthumously in 1850, the year after his death and presents the authors literary theory. Based on a series of lectures Poe had given late in his lifetime the essay argues that a poem should be written "for a poem's sake" and that the ultimate goal of art is aesthetic.

Poe tells you why he was against the concept of a long poem, saying that an epic, if it is to be worth anything, must instead be structured as a collection of shorter pieces, each of which is not too long to be read in a single sitting.

You'll discover why Poe considered didacticism the ultimate sin of the serious Poet and authors of Fiction.

This is followed by the controversial Poetic Principle (1846) where Poe elucidates a theory about how good writers write when they write well. He concludes that length, "unity of effect" and a logical method are important considerations for good writing. He also makes the assertion that "the death... of a beautiful woman" is "unquestionably the most poetical topic in the world". Poe deconstructs the exact process that led to his most startlingly gothic poem masterpiece "The Raven" as an example that his methods are sound.

Armed with his formidable advice and direction on how to write your very own Magnus Opus, his rare essay on Criticism is included here to help you deal with the reception of your own work and to correctly judge that of others.

Collected for the first time in one volume, the advice you receive from Poe cannot but improve your own writing skills.

If you absorb the wisdom and techniques of the Master of the Macabre, the Sensei of the Sensational, the ultimate of the unusual, then some of Poe's brilliance and magic is sure to illuminate your own literary ambitions.

TABLE OF CONTENTS

The Philosophy of Composition 1

The Poetic Principle 37

Criticism 97

The Raven 117

About the Author.......................................135

CHARLES DICKENS, in a note now lying before me, alluding to an examination I once made of the mechanism of "Barnaby Rudge," says- "By the way, are you aware that Godwin wrote his 'Caleb Williams' backwards? He first involved his hero in a web of difficulties, forming the second volume, and then, for the first, cast about him for some mode of accounting for what had been done."

I cannot think this the precise mode of procedure on the part of Godwin- and indeed what he himself acknowledges, is not altogether in accordance with Mr. Dickens' idea- but the author of "Caleb Williams" was too good an artist not to perceive the advantage derivable from at least a somewhat similar process. Nothing is more clear than that every plot, worth the name, must be elaborated to its denouement before anything be attempted with the pen. It is only with the denouement constantly in view that we can give a plot its indispensable air of consequence, or causation, by making the incidents, and especially the tone at all points, tend to the development of the intention.

There is a radical error, I think, in the usual mode of constructing a story. Either history affords a thesis- or one is suggested by an incident of the day- or, at best, the author sets himself to work in the combination of striking events to form merely the basis of his narrative-designing, generally, to fill in with description, dialogue, or autorial comment, whatever crevices of fact, or action, may, from page to page, render themselves apparent.

I prefer commencing with the consideration of an effect. Keeping originality always in view- for he is false to himself who ventures to dispense with so obvious and so easily attainable a source of interest- I say to myself, in the first place, "Of the innumerable effects, or impressions, of which the heart, the intellect, or (more generally) the soul is susceptible, what one shall I, on the present occasion, select?" Having chosen a novel, first, and secondly a vivid effect, I consider whether it can be best wrought by incident or tone- whether by ordinary incidents and peculiar tone, or the converse, or by peculiarity both of incident and tone- afterward looking about me (or rather within) for such combinations of event, or tone, as shall best aid me in the construction of the effect.

I have often thought how interesting a magazine paper might be written by any author who would- that is to say, who could- detail, step by step, the processes by which any one of his compositions attained its ultimate point of completion. Why such a paper has never been given to the world, I am much at a loss to say- but, perhaps, the autorial vanity has had more to do with the omission than any one other cause. Most writers- poets in especial- prefer having it understood that they compose by a species of fine frenzy- an ecstatic intuition- and would positively shudder at letting the public take a peep behind the scenes, at the elaborate and vacillating crudities of thought- at the true purposes seized only at the last moment- at the innumerable glimpses of idea that arrived not at the maturity of full view- at the fully-matured fancies discarded in despair as unmanageable- at the cautious selections and rejections- at the painful erasures and interpolations- in a word, at the wheels and pinions- the tackle for scene-shifting- the step-ladders, and demon-traps- the cock's feathers, the red paint and the black patches, which, in ninety-nine cases out of a hundred, constitute the properties of the literary histrio.

I am aware, on the other hand, that the case is by no means common, in which an author is at all in condition to retrace the steps by which his conclusions have been attained. In general, suggestions, having arisen pell-mell are pursued and forgotten in a similar manner.

For my own part, I have neither sympathy with the repugnance alluded to, nor, at any time, the least difficulty in recalling to mind the progressive steps of any of my compositions, and, since the interest of an analysis or reconstruction, such as I have considered a desideratum, is quite independent of any real or fancied interest in the thing analysed, it will not be regarded as a breach of decorum on my part to show the modus operandi by which some one of my own works was put together. I select 'The Raven' as most generally known. It is my design to render it manifest that no one point in its composition is referable either to accident or intuition- that the work proceeded step by step, to its completion, with the precision and rigid consequence of a mathematical problem.

Let us dismiss, as irrelevant to the poem, per se, the circumstance- or say the necessity- which, in the first place, gave rise to the intention of composing a poem that should suit at once the popular and the critical taste.

We commence, then, with this intention.

The initial consideration was that of extent. If any literary work is too long to be read at one sitting, we must be content to dispense with the immensely important effect derivable from unity of impression- for, if two sittings be required, the affairs of the world interfere, and everything like totality is at once destroyed. But since, ceteris paribus, no poet can afford to dispense with anything that may advance his design, it but remains to be seen whether there is, in extent, any advantage to counterbalance the loss of unity which attends it. Here I say no, at once. What we term a long poem is, in fact, merely a succession of brief ones- that is to say, of brief poetical effects. It is needless to demonstrate that a poem is such only inasmuch as it intensely excites, by elevating the soul; and all intense excitements are, through a psychal necessity, brief. For this reason, at least, one-half of the "Paradise Lost" is essentially prose- a succession of poetical excitements interspersed, inevitably, with corresponding depressions- the whole being deprived, through the extremeness of its length, of the vastly important artistic element, totality, or unity of effect.

It appears evident, then, that there is a distinct

limit, as regards length, to all works of literary art- the limit of a single sitting- and that, although in certain classes of prose composition, such as "Robinson Crusoe" (demanding no unity), this limit may be advantageously overpassed, it can never properly be overpassed in a poem. Within this limit, the extent of a poem may be made to bear mathematical relation to its merit- in other words, to the excitement or elevation-again, in other words, to the degree of the true poetical effect which it is capable of inducing; for it is clear that the brevity must be in direct ratio of the intensity of the intended effect- this, with one proviso- that a certain degree of duration is absolutely requisite for the production of any effect at all.

Holding in view these considerations, as well

as that degree of excitement which I deemed not above the popular, while not below the critical taste, I reached at once what I conceived the proper length for my intended poem- a length of about one hundred lines. It is, in fact, a hundred and eight.

My next thought concerned the choice of an impression, or effect, to be conveyed: and here I may as well observe that throughout the construction, I kept steadily in view the design of rendering the work universally appreciable. I should be carried too far out of my immediate topic were I to demonstrate a point upon which I have repeatedly insisted, and which, with the poetical, stands not in the slightest need of demonstration- the point, I mean, that Beauty is the sole legitimate province of the poem. A few words, however, in elucidation of my real meaning, which some of my friends have evinced a disposition to misrepresent. That pleasure which is at once the most intense, the most elevating, and the most pure is, I believe, found in the contemplation of the beautiful. When, indeed, men speak of Beauty, they mean, precisely, not a quality, as is supposed, but an effect- they refer, in short, just to that intense and pure elevation of soul- not of intellect, or of heart- upon which I have commented, and which is experienced in consequence of contemplating the "beautiful." Now I designate Beauty as the province of the poem, merely because it is an obvious rule of Art that effects should be made to spring from direct causes- that objects should be attained through means best adapted for their attainment- no one as yet having been weak enough to deny that the peculiar elevation alluded to is most readily attained in the poem. Now the object Truth, or the satisfaction of the intellect, and the object Passion, or the excitement of the heart, are, although attainable to a certain extent in poetry, far more readily attainable in prose. Truth, in fact, demands a precision, and Passion, a homeliness (the truly passionate will comprehend me), which are absolutely antagonistic to that Beauty which, I maintain, is the excitement or pleasurable elevation of the soul. It by no means follows, from anything here said, that passion, or even truth, may not be introduced, and even profitably introduced, into a poem for they may serve in elucidation, or aid the general effect, as do discords in music, by contrast- but the true artist will always contrive, first, to tone them into proper subservience to the predominant aim, and, secondly, to enveil them, as far as possible, in that Beauty which is the atmosphere and the essence of the poem.

Regarding, then, Beauty as my province, my next question referred to the tone of its highest manifestation- and all experience has shown that this tone is one of sadness. Beauty of whatever kind in its supreme development invariably excites the sensitive soul to tears. Melancholy is thus the most legitimate of all the poetical tones.

The length, the province, and the tone, being thus determined, I betook myself to ordinary induction, with the view of obtaining some artistic piquancy which might serve me as a key-note in the construction of the poem- some pivot upon which the whole structure might turn. In carefully thinking over all the usual artistic effects- or more properly points, in the theatrical sense- I did not fail to perceive immediately that no one had been so universally employed as that of the refrain. The universality of its employment sufficed to assure me of its intrinsic value, and spared me the necessity of submitting it to analysis. I considered it, however, with regard to its susceptibility of improvement, and soon saw it to be in a primitive condition. As commonly used, the refrain, or burden, not only is limited to lyric verse, but depends for its impression upon the force of monotone- both in sound and thought. The pleasure is deduced solely from the sense of identity- of repetition. I resolved to diversify, and so heighten the effect, by adhering in general to the monotone of sound, while I continually varied that of thought: that is to say, I determined to produce continuously novel effects, by the variation of the application of the refrain- the refrain itself remaining for the most part, unvaried.

These points being settled, I next bethought me of the nature of my refrain. Since its application was to be repeatedly varied it was clear that the refrain itself must be brief, for there would have been an insurmountable difficulty in frequent variations of application in any sentence of length. In proportion to the brevity of the sentence would, of course, be the facility of the variation. This led me at once to a single word as the best refrain.

The question now arose as to the character of the word. Having made up my mind to a refrain, the division of the poem into stanzas was of course a corollary, the refrain forming the close to each stanza. That such a close, to have force, must be sonorous and susceptible of protracted emphasis, admitted no doubt, and these considerations inevitably led me to the long o as the most sonorous vowel in connection with r as the most producible consonant.

The sound of the refrain being thus determined, it became necessary to select a word embodying this sound, and at the same time in the fullest possible keeping with that melancholy which I had pre-determined as the tone of the poem. In such a search it would have been absolutely impossible to overlook the word "Nevermore." In fact it was the very first which presented itself.

The next desideratum was a pretext for the continuous use of the one word "nevermore." In observing the difficulty which I had at once found in inventing a sufficiently plausible reason for its continuous repetition, I did not fail to perceive that this difficulty arose solely from the preassumption that the word was to be so continuously or monotonously spoken by a human being- I did not fail to perceive, in short, that the difficulty lay in the reconciliation of this monotony with the exercise of reason on the part of the creature repeating the word. Here, then, immediately arose the idea of a non-reasoning creature capable of speech, and very naturally, a parrot, in the first instance, suggested itself, but was superseded forthwith by a Raven as equally capable of speech, and infinitely more in keeping with the intended tone.

I had now gone so far as the conception of a Raven, the bird of ill-omen, monotonously repeating the one word "Nevermore" at the conclusion of each stanza in a poem of melancholy tone, and in length about one hundred lines. Now, never losing sight of the object- supremeness or perfection at all points, I asked myself- "Of all melancholy topics what, according to the universal understanding of mankind, is the most melancholy?" Death, was the obvious reply. "And when," I said, "is this most melancholy of topics most poetical?" From what I have already explained at some length the answer here also is obvious- "When it most closely allies itself to Beauty: the death then of a beautiful woman is unquestionably the most poetical topic in the world, and equally is it beyond doubt that the lips best suited for such topic are those of a bereaved lover."

I had now to combine the two ideas of a lover lamenting his deceased mistress and a Raven continuously repeating the word "Nevermore." I had to combine these, bearing in mind my design of varying at every turn the application of the word repeated, but the only intelligible mode of such combination is that of imagining the Raven employing the word in answer to the queries of the lover. And here it was that I saw at once the opportunity afforded for the effect on which I had been depending, that is to say, the effect of the variation of application. I saw that I could make the first query propounded by the lover- the first query to which the Raven should reply "Nevermore"- that I could make this first query a commonplace one, the second less so, the third still less, and so on, until at length the lover, startled from his original nonchalance by the melancholy character of the word itself, by its frequent repetition, and by a consideration of the ominous reputation of the fowl that uttered it, is at length excited to superstition, and wildly propounds queries of a far different character- queries whose solution he has passionately at heart- propounds them half in superstition and half in that species of despair which delights in self-torture- propounds them not altogether because he believes in the prophetic or demoniac character of the bird (which reason assures him is merely repeating a lesson learned by rote), but because he experiences a frenzied pleasure in so modelling his questions as to receive from the expected "Nevermore" the most delicious because the most intolerable of sorrows. Perceiving the opportunity thus afforded me, or, more strictly, thus forced upon me in the progress of the construction, I first established in my mind the climax or concluding query- that query to which "Nevermore" should be in the last place an answer- that query in reply to which this word "Nevermore" should involve the utmost conceivable amount of sorrow and despair.

Here then the poem may be said to have had its beginning- at the end where all works of art should begin- for it was here at this point of my preconsiderations that I first put pen to paper in the composition of the stanza:

"Prophet!" said I, "thing of evil! prophet still if bird or devil!

By that Heaven that bends above us- by that God we both adore,

Tell this soul with sorrow laden, if, within the distant Aidenn,

It shall clasp a sainted maiden whom the angels name Lenore-

Clasp a rare and radiant maiden whom the angels name Lenore."

Quoth the Raven- "Nevermore."

I composed this stanza, at this point, first that, by establishing the climax, I might the better vary and graduate, as regards seriousness and importance, the preceding queries of the lover, and secondly, that I might definitely settle the rhythm, the metre, and the length and general arrangement of the stanza, as well as graduate the stanzas which were to precede, so that none of them might surpass this in rhythmical effect. Had I been able in the subsequent composition to construct more vigorous stanzas I should without scruple have purposely enfeebled them so as not to interfere with the climacteric effect.

And here I may as well say a few words of the versification. My first object (as usual) was originality. The extent to which this has been neglected in versification is one of the most unaccountable things in the world. Admitting that there is little possibility of variety in mere rhythm, it is still clear that the possible varieties of metre and stanza are absolutely infinite, and yet, for centuries, no man, in verse, has ever done, or ever seemed to think of doing, an original thing. The fact is that originality (unless in minds of very unusual force) is by no means a matter, as some suppose, of impulse or intuition. In general, to be found, it must be elaborately sought, and although a positive merit of the highest class, demands in its attainment less of invention than negation.

Of course I pretend to no originality in either the rhythm or metre of the "Raven." The former is trochaic- the latter is octametre acatalectic, alternating with heptametre catalectic repeated in the refrain of the fifth verse, and terminating with tetrametre catalectic. Less pedantically the feet employed throughout (trochees) consist of a long syllable followed by a short, the first line of the stanza consists of eight of these feet, the second of seven and a half (in effect two-thirds), the third of eight, the fourth of seven and a half, the fifth the same, the sixth three and a half. Now, each of these lines taken individually has been employed before, and what originality the "Raven" has, is in their combination into stanza; nothing even remotely approaching this has ever been attempted. The effect of this originality of combination is aided by other unusual and some altogether novel effects, arising from an extension of the application of the principles of rhyme and alliteration.

The next point to be considered was the mode of bringing together the lover and the Raven- and the first branch of this consideration was the locale. For this the most natural suggestion might seem to be a forest, or the fields- but it has always appeared to me that a close circumscription of space is absolutely necessary to the effect of insulated incident- it has the force of a frame to a picture. It has an indisputable moral power in keeping concentrated the attention, and, of course, must not be confounded with mere unity of place.

I determined, then, to place the lover in his chamber- in a chamber rendered sacred to him by memories of her who had frequented it. The room is represented as richly furnished- this in mere pursuance of the ideas I have already explained on the subject of Beauty, as the sole true poetical thesis.

The locale being thus determined, I had now to introduce the bird- and the thought of introducing him through the window was inevitable. The idea of making the lover suppose, in the first instance, that the flapping of the wings of the bird against the shutter, is a "tapping" at the door, originated in a wish to increase, by prolonging, the reader's curiosity, and in a desire to admit the incidental effect arising from the lover's throwing open the door, finding all dark, and thence adopting the half-fancy that it was the spirit of his mistress that knocked.

I made the night tempestuous, first to account for the Raven's seeking admission, and secondly, for the effect of contrast with the (physical) serenity within the chamber.

I made the bird alight on the bust of Pallas, also for the effect of contrast between the marble and the plumage- it being understood that the bust was absolutely suggested by the bird- the bust of Pallas being chosen, first, as most in keeping with the scholarship of the lover, and secondly, for the sonorousness of the word, Pallas, itself.

About the middle of the poem, also, I have availed myself of the force of contrast, with a view of deepening the ultimate impression. For example, an air of the fantastic- approaching as nearly to the ludicrous as was admissible- is given to the Raven's entrance. He comes in "with many a flirt and flutter."

Not the least obeisance made he- not a moment stopped or stayed he,

But with mien of lord or lady, perched above my chamber door.

In the two stanzas which follow, the design is more obviously carried out:-

Then this ebony bird, beguiling my sad fancy into smiling

By the grave and stern decorum of the countenance it wore,

"Though thy crest be shorn and shaven, thou," I said, "art sure no

craven,

Ghastly grim and ancient Raven wandering from the Nightly shore-

Tell me what thy lordly name is on the Night's Plutonian shore?"

    Quoth the Raven- "Nevermore."

Much I marvelled this ungainly fowl to hear discourse so plainly,

Though its answer little meaning- little relevancy bore;

For we cannot help agreeing that no living human being

Ever yet was blessed with seeing bird above his chamber door-

Bird or beast upon the sculptured bust above his chamber door,

    With such name as "Nevermore."

The effect of the denouement being thus provided for, I immediately drop the fantastic for a tone of the most profound seriousness- this tone commencing in the stanza directly following the one last quoted, with the line,

But the Raven, sitting lonely on that placid bust, spoke only, etc.

From this epoch the lover no longer jests- no longer sees anything even of the fantastic in the Raven's demeanour. He speaks of him as a "grim, ungainly, ghastly, gaunt, and ominous bird of yore," and feels the "fiery eyes" burning into his "bosom's core." This revolution of thought, or fancy, on the lover's part, is intended to induce a similar one on the part of the reader- to bring the mind into a proper frame for the denouement- which is now brought about as rapidly and as directly as possible.

With the denouement proper- with the Raven's reply, "Nevermore," to the lover's final demand if he shall meet his mistress in another world- the poem, in its obvious phase, that of a simple narrative, may be said to have its completion. So far, everything is within the limits of the accountable- of the real. A raven, having learned by rote the single word "Nevermore," and having escaped from the custody of its owner, is driven at midnight, through the violence of a storm, to seek admission at a window from which a light still gleams- the chamber-window of a student, occupied half in poring over a volume, half in dreaming of a beloved mistress deceased. The casement being thrown open at the fluttering of the bird's wings, the bird itself perches on the most convenient seat out of the immediate reach of the student, who amused by the incident and the oddity of the visitor's demeanour, demands of it, in jest and without looking for a reply, its name. The raven addressed, answers with its customary word, "Nevermore"- a word which finds immediate echo in the melancholy heart of the student, who, giving utterance aloud to certain thoughts suggested by the occasion, is again startled by the fowl's repetition of "Nevermore." The student now guesses the state of the case, but is impelled, as I have before explained, by the human thirst for self-torture, and in part by superstition, to propound such queries to the bird as will bring him, the lover, the most of the luxury of sorrow, through the anticipated answer, "Nevermore." With the indulgence, to the extreme, of this self-torture, the narration, in what I have termed its first or obvious phase, has a natural termination, and so far there has been no overstepping of the limits of the real.

But in subjects so handled, however skillfully, or with however vivid an array of incident, there is always a certain hardness or nakedness which repels the artistical eye. Two things are invariably required- first, some amount of complexity, or more properly, adaptation; and, secondly, some amount of suggestiveness- some under-current, however indefinite, of meaning. It is this latter, in especial, which imparts to a work of art so much of that richness (to borrow from colloquy a forcible term), which we are too fond of confounding with the ideal. It is the excess of the suggested meaning- it is the rendering this the upper

instead of the under-current of the theme-
which turns into prose (and that of the very
flattest kind), the so-called poetry of the so-
called transcendentalists.

Holding these opinions, I added the two
concluding stanzas of the poem- their
suggestiveness being thus made to pervade all
the narrative which has preceded them. The
under-current of meaning is rendered first
apparent in the line-

*"Take thy beak from out my heart, and take
thy form from off my*
door!"
Quoth the Raven "Nevermore!"

It will be observed that the words, "from out
my heart," involve the first metaphorical

expression in the poem. They, with the answer, "Nevermore," dispose the mind to seek a moral in all that has been previously narrated. The reader begins now to regard the Raven as emblematical- but it is not until the very last line of the very last stanza that the intention of making him emblematical of Mournful and never ending Remembrance is permitted distinctly to be seen:

And the Raven, never flitting, still is sitting, still is sitting,
 On the pallid bust of Pallas just above my chamber door;
 And his eyes have all the seeming of a demon that is dreaming,
 And the lamplight o'er him streaming throws his shadow on the floor;

*And my soul from out that shadow that lies
floating on the floor
        Shall be lifted- nevermore.*

The Poetic Principle

IN SPEAKING of the Poetic Principle, I have no design to be either thorough or profound. While discussing, very much at random, the essentiality of what we call Poetry, my principal purpose will be to cite for consideration, some few of those minor English or American poems which best suit my own taste, or which, upon my own fancy, have left the most definite impression. By "minor poems" I mean, of course, poems of little length. And here, in the beginning, permit me to say a few words in regard to a somewhat peculiar principle, which, whether rightfully or wrongfully, has always had its influence in my own critical estimate of the poem. I hold that a

long poem does not exist. I maintain that the
phrase, "a long poem," is simply a flat
contradiction in terms.

I need scarcely observe that a poem deserves
its title only inasmuch as it excites, by elevating
the soul. The value of the poem is in the ratio
of this elevating excitement. But all excitements
are, through a psychal necessity, transient.
That degree of excitement which would entitle
a poem to be so called at all, cannot be
sustained throughout a composition of any
great length. After the lapse of half an hour, at
the very utmost, it flags- fails- a revulsion
ensues- and then the poem is, in effect and in
fact, no longer such.

There are, no doubt, many who have found
difficulty in reconciling the critical dictum that

the "Paradise Lost" is to be devoutly admired throughout, with the absolute impossibility of maintaining for it, during perusal, the amount of enthusiasm which that critical dictum would demand. This great work, in fact, is to be regarded as poetical, only when, losing sight of that vital requisite in all works of Art, Unity, we view it merely as a series of minor poems. If, to preserve its Unity- its totality of effect or impression- we read it (as would be necessary) at a single sitting, the result is but a constant alteration of excitement and depression. After a passage of what we feel to be true poetry, there follows, inevitably, a passage of platitude which no critical prejudgment can force us to admire; but if, upon completing the work, we read it again, omitting the first book- that is to say, commencing with the second- we shall be surprised at now finding that admirable which we before condemned- that damnable which we had previously so much admired. It follows from all this that the ultimate, aggregate, or absolute effect of even the best epic under the sun, is a nullity:- and this is precisely the fact.

In regard to the Iliad, we have, if not positive proof, at least very good reason for believing it intended as a series of lyrics; but, granting the epic intention, I can say only that the work is based in an imperfect sense of art. The modern epic is, of the supposititious ancient model, but an inconsiderate and blindfold imitation. But the day of these artistic anomalies is over. If, at any time, any very long poem were popular in reality, which I doubt, it is at least clear that no very long poem will ever be popular again.

That the extent of a poetical work is, ceteris

paribus, the measure of its merit, seems undoubtedly, when we thus state it a proposition sufficiently absurd- yet we are indebted for it to the Quarterly Reviews. Surely there can be nothing in mere size, abstractly considered- there can be nothing in mere bulk, so far as a volume is concerned, which has so continuously elicited admiration from these saturnine pamphlets! A mountain, to be sure, by the mere sentiment of physical magnitude which it conveys, does impress us with a sense of the sublime- but no man is impressed after this fashion by the material grandeur of even "The Columbiad." Even the Quarterlies have not instructed us to be so impressed by it. As yet, they have not insisted on our estimating Lamartine by the cubic foot, or Pollock by the pound- but what else are we to infer from their continual prating about "sustained effort"? If, by "sustained effort," any little gentleman has accomplished an epic, let us frankly commend him for the effort- if this indeed be a thing commendable- but let us forbear praising the epic on the effort's account. It is to be hoped that common sense, in the time to come, will prefer deciding upon a work of Art rather by the impression it makes- by the effect it produces- than by the time it took to impress the effect, or by the amount of "sustained effort" which had been found necessary in effecting the impression. The fact is, that perseverance is one thing and genius quite another- nor can all the Quarterlies in Christendom confound them. By and by, this proposition, with many which I have been just urging, will be received as self-evident. In the meantime, by being generally condemned as falsities, they will not be essentially damaged as truths.

On the other hand, it is clear that a poem may be improperly brief. Undue brevity degenerates into mere epigrammatism. A very short poem, while now and then producing a brilliant or vivid, never produces a profound or enduring effect. There must be the steady pressing down of the stamp upon the wax. De Beranger has wrought innumerable things, pungent and spirit-stirring, but in general they have been too imponderous to stamp themselves deeply into the public attention, and thus, as so many feathers of fancy, have been blown aloft only to be whistled down the wind.

A remarkable instance of the effect of undue brevity in depressing a poem, in keeping it out of the popular view, is afforded by the following exquisite little Serenade-

I arise from dreams of thee
  In the first sweet sleep of night,
  When the winds are breathing low,
  And the stars are shining bright.
I arise from dreams of thee,
  And a spirit in my feet
Has led me- who knows how?-
  To thy chamber-window, sweet!

The wandering airs they faint
  On the dark the silent stream-
The champak odors fail
  Like sweet thoughts in a dream;

The nightingale's complaint,
  It dies upon her heart,
As I must die on thine,
  O, beloved as thou art!

O, lift me from the grass!
  I die, I faint, I fail!
Let thy love in kisses rain
  On my lips and eyelids pale.
My cheek is cold and white, alas!
  My heart beats loud and fast:
O, press it close to thine again,
  Where it will break at last.

Very few perhaps are familiar with these lines-
yet no less a poet than Shelley is their author.
Their warm, yet delicate and ethereal
imagination will be appreciated by all, but by
none so thoroughly as by him who has himself

arisen from sweet dreams of one beloved to bathe in the aromatic air of a southern midsummer night.

One of the finest poems by Willis- the very best in my opinion which he has ever written- has no doubt, through this same defect of undue brevity, been kept back from its proper position, not less in the critical than in the popular view:-

The shadows lay along Broadway, 'Twas near the twilight-tide- And slowly there a lady fair Was walking in her pride. Alone walk'd she; but, viewlessly, Walk'd spirits at her side. Peace charm'd the street beneath her feet, And Honour charm'd the air, And all astir looked kind on her, And called her good as fair- For all God ever gave to her She kept with chary care. She kept with care her beauties rare From lovers warm and true- For heart was cold to all but gold, And the rich came not to woo- But honour'd well her charms to sell If priests the selling do. Now walking there was one more fair- A slight girl lily-pale; And she had unseen company To make the spirit quail- 'Twixt Want and Scorn she walk'd forlorn, And nothing could avail. No mercy now can clear her brow From this world's peace to pray, For as loves wild prayer dissolved in air, Her woman's heart gave way!- But the sin forgiven by Christ in Heaven, By man is cursed alway!

In this composition we find it difficult to recognise the Willis who has written so many mere "verses of society." The lines are not only richly ideal, but full of energy, while they breathe an earnestness, an evident sincerity of sentiment, for which we look in vain throughout all the other works of this author.

While the epic mania, while the idea that to merit in poetry prolixity is indispensable, has for some years past been gradually dying out of the public mind, by mere dint of its own absurdity, we find it succeeded by a heresy too palpably false to be long tolerated, but one which, in the brief period it has already endured, may be said to have accomplished more in the corruption of our Poetical Literature than all its other enemies combined. I allude to the heresies of The Didactic. It has been assumed, tacitly and avowedly, directly and indirectly, that the ultimate object of all Poetry is Truth. Every poem, it is said, should inculcate a moral, and by this moral is the poetical merit of the work to be adjudged. We

Americans especially have patronized this happy idea, and we Bostonians very especially have developed it in full. We have taken it into our heads that to write a poem simply for the poem's sake, and to acknowledge such to have been our design, would be to confess ourselves radically wanting in the true poetic dignity and force:- but the simple fact is that would we but permit ourselves to look into our own souls we should immediately there discover that under the sun there neither exists nor can exist any work more thoroughly dignified, more supremely noble, than this very poem, this poem per se, this poem which is a poem and nothing more, this poem written solely for the poem's sake.

With as deep a reverence for the True as ever inspired the bosom of man, I would nevertheless limit, in some measure, its modes of inculcation. I would limit to enforce them. I would not enfeeble them by dissipation. The demands of Truth are severe. She has no sympathy with the myrtles. All that which is so indispensable in Song is precisely all that with which she has nothing whatever to do. It is but making her a flaunting paradox to wreathe her in gems and flowers. In enforcing a truth we need severity rather than efflorescence of language. We must be simple, precise, terse. We must be cool, calm, unimpassioned. In a word, we must be in that mood which, as nearly as possible, is the exact converse of the poetical. He must be blind indeed who does not perceive the radical and chasmal difference between the truthful and the poetical modes of inculcation. He must be theory-mad beyond redemption who, in spite of these differences, shall still persist in attempting to reconcile the obstinate oils and waters of Poetry and Truth.

Dividing the world of mind into its three most immediately obvious distinctions, we have the Pure Intellect, Taste, and the Moral Sense. I place Taste in the middle, because it is just this position which in the mind it occupies. It holds intimate relations with either extreme; but from the Moral Sense is separated by so faint a difference that Aristotle has not hesitated to place some of its operations among the virtues themselves. Nevertheless we find the offices of the trio marked with a sufficient distinction. Just as the Intellect concerns itself with Truth, so Taste informs us of the Beautiful, while the Moral Sense is regardful of Duty. Of this latter, while Conscience teaches the obligation, and Reason the expediency, Taste contents herself

with displaying the charms:- waging war upon
Vice solely on the ground of her deformity- her
disproportion- her animosity to the fitting, to
the appropriate, to the harmonious- in a word,
to Beauty.

An immortal instinct deep within the spirit of
man is thus plainly a sense of the Beautiful.
This it is which administers to his delight in the
manifold forms, and sounds, and odors and
sentiments amid which he exists. And just as
the lily is repeated in the lake, or the eyes of
Amaryllis in the mirror, so is the mere oral or
written repetition of these forms, and sounds,
and colors, and odors, and sentiments a
duplicate source of delight. But this mere
repetition is not poetry. He who shall simply
sing, with however glowing enthusiasm, or
with however vivid a truth of description, of

the sights, and sounds, and odors, and colors, and sentiments which greet him in common with all mankind- he, I say, has yet faded to prove his divine title. There is still a something in the distance which he has been unable to attain. We have still a thirst unquenchable, to allay which he has not shown us the crystal springs. This thirst belongs to the immortality of Man. It is at once a consequence and an indication of his perennial existence. It is the desire of the moth for the star. It is no mere appreciation of the Beauty before us, but a wild effort to reach the Beauty above. Inspired by an ecstatic prescience of the glories beyond the grave, we struggle by multiform combinations among the things and thoughts of Time to attain a portion of that Loveliness whose very elements perhaps appertain to eternity alone. And thus when by Poetry, or when by Music, the most entrancing of the poetic moods, we find ourselves melted into tears, we weep then, not as the Abbate Gravina supposes, through excess of pleasure, but through a certain petulant, impatient sorrow at our inability to grasp now, wholly, here on earth, at once and for ever, those divine and rapturous joys of which through the poem, or through the music, we attain to but brief and indeterminate glimpses.

The struggle to apprehend the supernal Loveliness- this struggle, on the part of souls fittingly constituted- has given to the world all that which it (the world) has ever been enabled at once to understand and to feel as poetic.

The Poetic Sentiment, of course, may develop

itself in various modes- in Painting, in Sculpture, in Architecture, in the Dance- very especially in Music- and very peculiarly, and with a wide field, in the composition of the Landscape Garden. Our present theme, however, has regard only to its manifestation in words. And here let me speak briefly on the topic of rhythm. Contenting myself with the certainty that Music, in its various modes of metre, rhythm, and rhyme, is of so vast a moment in Poetry as never to be wisely rejected- is so vitally important an adjunct that he is simply silly who declines its assistance, I will not now pause to maintain its absolute essentiality. It is in Music perhaps that the soul most nearly attains the great end for which, when inspired by the Poetic Sentiment it struggles- the creation of supernal Beauty. It may be, indeed, that here this sublime end is, now and then, attained in fact. We are often made to feel, with a shivering delight, that from an earthly harp are stricken notes which cannot have been unfamiliar to the angels. And thus there can be little doubt that in the union of Poetry with Music in its popular sense, we shall find the widest field for the Poetic development. The old Bards and Minnesingers had advantages which we do not possess- and Thomas Moore, singing his own songs, was, in the most legitimate manner, perfecting them as poems.

To recapitulate then:- I would define, in brief, the Poetry of words as The Rhythmical Creation of Beauty. Its sole arbiter is Taste. With the Intellect or with the Conscience it has only collateral relations. Unless incidentally, it has no concern whatever either with Duty or with Truth.

A few words, however, in explanation. That pleasure which is at once the most pure, the most elevating, and the most intense, is derived, I maintain, from the contemplation of the Beautiful. In the contemplation of Beauty we alone find it possible to attain that pleasurable elevation, or excitement of the soul, which we recognise as the Poetic Sentiment, and which is so easily distinguished from Truth, which is the satisfaction of the Reason, or from Passion, which is the excitement of the heart. I make Beauty, therefore- using the word as inclusive of the sublime- I make Beauty the province of the poem, simply because it is an obvious rule of Art that effects should be made to spring as directly as possible from their causes:- no one as yet having been weak enough to deny that the peculiar elevation in question is at least most readily attainable in the poem. It by no means follows, however, that the incitements of Passion, or the precepts of Duty, or even the lessons of Truth, may not be introduced into a poem, and with advantage, for they may subserve incidentally, in various ways, the general purposes of the work: but the true artist will always contrive to tone them down in proper subjection to that Beauty which is the atmosphere and the real essence of the poem.

I cannot better introduce the few poems which I shall present for your consideration, than by the citation of the Proem to Longfellow's "Waif":-

The day is done, and the darkness
  Falls from the wings of Night,
As a feather is wafted downward
  From an Eagle in his flight.

I see the lights of the village
  Gleam through the rain and the mist,
And a feeling of sadness comes o'er me,
  That my soul cannot resist;

A feeling of sadness and longing,
  That is not akin to pain,
And resembles sorrow only
  As the mist resembles the rain.

Come, read to me some poem,
  Some simple and heartfelt lay,
That shall soothe this restless feeling,

And banish the thoughts of day.

Not from the grand old masters,
 Not from the bards sublime,
Whose distant footsteps echo
 Through the corridors of Time.

For, like strains of martial music,
 Their mighty thoughts suggest
Life's endless toil and endeavour;
 And to-night I long for rest.

Read from some humbler poet,
 Whose songs gushed from his heart,
As showers from the clouds of summer,
 Or tears from the eyelids start;

Who through long days of labor,
 And nights devoid of ease,

Still heard in his soul the music
  Of wonderful melodies.

Such songs have power to quiet
  The restless pulse of care,
And come like the benediction
  That follows after prayer.

Then read from the treasured volume
  The poem of thy choice,
And lend to the rhyme of the poet
  The beauty of thy voice.

And the night shall be filled with music,
  And the cares that infest the day
Shall fold their tents like the Arabs,
  And as silently steal away.
With no great range of imagination, these lines
have been justly admired for their delicacy of

expression. Some of the images are very effective. Nothing can be better than-
-the bards sublime,
Whose distant footsteps echo
Down the corridors of Time.

The idea of the last quatrain is also very effective. The poem on the whole, however, is chiefly to be admired for the graceful insouciance of its metre, so well in accordance with the character of the sentiments, and especially for the ease of the general manner. This "ease" or naturalness, in a literary style, it has long been the fashion to regard as ease in appearance alone- as a point of really difficult attainment. But not so:- a natural manner is difficult only to him who should never meddle with it- to the unnatural. It is but the result of writing with the understanding, or with the instinct, that the tone, in composition, should always be that which the mass of mankind would adopt- and must perpetually vary, of course, with the occasion. The author who, after the fashion of "The North American Review," should be upon all occasions merely "quiet," must necessarily upon many occasions be simply silly, or stupid; and has no more right to be considered "easy" or "natural" than a Cockney exquisite, or than the sleeping Beauty in the waxworks.

Among the minor poems of Bryant, none has so much impressed me as the one which he entitles "June." I quote only a portion of it:-

There, through the long, long summer hours,
The golden light should lie,

And thick young herbs and groups of
flowers
   Stand in their beauty by.
The oriole should build and tell
His love-tale, close beside my cell;
   The idle butterfly
Should rest him there, and there be heard
The housewife-bee and humming bird.

And what if cheerful shouts at noon,
   Come, from the village sent,
Or songs of maids, beneath the moon,
   With fairy laughter blent?
And what if, in the evening light,
Betrothed lovers walk in sight
   Of my low monument?
I would the lovely scene around
Might know no sadder sight nor sound.

I know, I know I should not see
  The season's glorious show,
Nor would its brightness shine for me;
  Nor its wild music flow;
But if, around my place of sleep,
The friends I love should come to weep,
  They might not haste to go.
Soft airs and song, and the light and
bloom,
  Should keep them lingering by my tomb.

These to their soften'd hearts should bear
  The thoughts of what has been,
And speak of one who cannot share
  The gladness of the scene;
Whose part in all the pomp that fills
The circuit of the summer hills,
  Is- that his grave is green;
And deeply would their hearts rejoice

To hear again his living voice.

The rhythmical flow here is even voluptuous-
nothing could be more melodious. The poem
has always affected me in a remarkable
manner. The intense melancholy which seems
to well up, perforce, to the surface of all the
poet's cheerful sayings about his grave, we find
thrilling us to the soul- while there is the truest
poetic elevation in the thrill. The impression
left is one of a pleasurable sadness. And if, in
the remaining compositions which I shall
introduce to you, there be more or less of a
similar tone always apparent, let me remind
you that (how or why we know not) this
certain taint of sadness is inseparably
connected with all the higher manifestations of
true Beauty. It is, nevertheless,

A feeling of sadness and longing
* That is not akin to pain,*
And resembles sorrow only
* As the mist resembles the rain.*

The taint of which I speak is clearly perceptible even in a poem so full of brilliancy and spirit as "The Health" of Edward Coate Pinckney:-

I fill this cup to one made up
* Of loveliness alone,*
A woman, of her gentle sex
* The seeming paragon;*
To whom the better elements
* And kindly stars have given*
A form so fair that, like the air,
* 'Tis less of earth than heaven.*

Her every tone is musies own,

Like those of morning birds,
And something more than melody
   Dwells ever in her words;
The coinage of her heart are they,
   And from her lips each flows
As one may see the burden'd be
   Forth issue from the rose.

Affections are as thoughts to her,
   The measures of her hours;
Her feelings have the fragrancy,
   The freshness of young flowers;
And lovely passions, changing oft,
   So fill her, she appears
The image of themselves by turns,
   The idol of past years!

Of her bright face one glance will trace
   A picture on the brain,

And of her voice in echoing hearts
  A sound must long remain;
But memory, such as mine of her,
  So very much endears
When death is nigh my latest sigh
  Will not be life's, but hers.

I fill'd this cup to one made up
  Of loveliness alone,
A woman, of her gentle sex
  The seeming paragon-
Her health! and would on earth there
stood,
  Some more of such a frame,
  That life might be all poetry,
  And weariness a name.

It was the misfortune of Mr. Pinckney to have
been born too far south. Had he been a New

Englander, it is probable that he would have been ranked as the first of American lyrists by that magnanimous cabal which has so long controlled the destinies of American Letters, in conducting the thing called "The North American Review." The poem just cited is especially beautiful; but the poetic elevation which it induces we must refer chiefly to our sympathy in the poet's enthusiasm. We pardon his hyperboles for the evident earnestness with which they are uttered.

It was by no means my design, however, to expatiate upon the merits of what I should read you. These will necessarily speak for themselves. Boccalini, in his "Advertisements from Parnassus," tells us that Zoilus once presented Apollo a very caustic criticism upon a very admirable book:- whereupon the god asked him for the beauties of the work. He replied that he only busied himself about the errors. On hearing this, Apollo, handing him a sack of unwinnowed wheat, bade him pick out all the chaff for his reward.

Now this fable answers very well as a hit at the critics- but I am by no means sure that the god was in the right. I am by no means certain that the true limits of the critical duty are not grossly misunderstood. Excellence, in a poem especially, may be considered in the light of an axiom, which need only be properly put, to become self-evident. It is not excellence if it require to be demonstrated as such:- and thus to point out too particularly the merits of a work of Art, is to admit that they are not merits altogether.

Among the "Melodies" of Thomas Moore is one

whose distinguished character as a poem proper seems to have been singularly left out of view. I allude to his lines beginning- "Come, rest in this bosom." The intense energy of their expression is not surpassed by anything in Byron. There are two of the lines in which a sentiment is conveyed that embodies the all in all of the divine passion of Love- a sentiment which, perhaps, has found its echo in more, and in more passionate, human hearts than any other single sentiment ever embodied in words:-

Come, rest in this bosom, my own stricken deer
Though the herd have fled from thee, thy home is still here;
Here still is the smile, that no cloud can o'ercast,

And a heart and a hand all thy own to the last.

Oh! what was love made for, if 'tis not the same
Through joy and through torment, through glory and shame?
I know not, I ask not, if guilt's in that heart,
I but know that I love thee, whatever thou art.

Thou hast call'd me thy Angel in moments of bliss,
And thy Angel I'll be, 'mid the horrors of this,-
Through the furnace, unshrinking, thy steps to pursue,

And shield thee, and save thee,- or perish
there tool

It has been the fashion of late days to deny
Moore Imagination, while granting him Fancy-
a distinction originating with Coleridge- than
whom no man more fully comprehended the
great powers of Moore. The fact is, that the
fancy of this poet so far predominates over all
his other faculties, and over the fancy of all
other men, as to have induced, very naturally,
the idea that he is fanciful only. But never was
there a greater mistake. Never was a grosser
wrong done the fame of a true poet. In the
compass of the English language I can call to
mind no poem more profoundly- more weirdly
imaginative, in the best sense, than the lines
commencing- "I would I were by that dim
lake"- which are the composition of Thomas

Moore. I regret that I am unable to remember them.

One of the noblest- and, speaking of Fancy- one of the most singularly fanciful of modern poets, was Thomas Hood. His "Fair Ines" had always for me an inexpressible charm:-

O saw ye not fair Ines?
  She's gone into the West,
To dazzle when the sun is down,
  And rob the world of rest;
She took our daylight with her,
  The smiles that we love best,
With morning blushes on her cheek,
  And pearls upon her breast.

O turn again, fair Ines,
  Before the fall of night,

For fear the moon should shine alone,
   And stars unrivall'd bright;
And blessed will the lover be
   That walks beneath their light,
And breathes the love against thy cheek
   I dare not even write!

Would I had been, fair Ines,
   That gallant cavalier,
Who rode so gaily by thy side,
   And whisper'd thee so near!
Were there no bonny dames at home
   Or no true lovers here,
That he should cross the seas to win
   The dearest of the dear?

I saw thee, lovely Ines,
   Descend along the shore,
With bands of noble gentlemen,

And banners waved before,
And gentle youth and maidens gay,
  And snowy plumes they wore;
It would have been a beauteous dream,
  If it had been no more!

Alas, alas, fair Ines,
  She went away with song,
With music waiting on her steps,
  And shoutings of the throng;
But some were sad and felt no mirth,
  But only Music's wrong,
In sounds that sang Farewell, Farewell,
  To her you've loved so long.

Farewell, farewell, fair Ines,
  That vessel never bore
So fair a lady on its deck,
  Nor danced so light before,-

Alas for pleasure on the sea,
  And sorrow on the shore!
The smile that blest one lover's heart
  Has broken many more!

"The Haunted House," by the same author, is one of the truest poems ever written,- one of the truest, one of the most unexceptionable, one of the most thoroughly artistic, both in its theme and in its execution. It is, moreover, powerfully ideal- imaginative. I regret that its length renders it unsuitable for the purposes of this lecture. In place of it permit me to offer the universally appreciated "Bridge of Sighs":-

One more Unfortunate,
Weary of breath,
Gone to her death!

Take her up tenderly,
Lift her with care,-
Fashion'd so slenderly,
Young and so fair!

Look at her garments
Clinging like cerements;
Whilst the wave constantly
Drips from her clothing;
Take her up instantly,
Loving, not loathing.

Touch her not scornfully,
Think of her mournfully,
Gently and humanly,
Not of the stains of her,
All that remains of her
Now is pure womanly.

Make no deep scrutiny
Into her mutiny
Rash and undutiful;
Past all dishonor,
Death has left on her
Only the beautiful.

Where the lamps quiver
So far in the river,
With many a light
From window and casement
From garret to basement,
She stood, with amazement,
Houseless by night

The bleak wind of March
Made her tremble and shiver,
But not the dark arch,
Or the black flowing river:

Mad from life's history,
Glad to death's mystery,
Swift to be hurl'd-
Anywhere, anywhere
Out of the world!

In she plunged boldly,
No matter how coldly
The rough river ran,-
Over the brink of it,
Picture it,- think of it,
Dissolute Man!
Lave in it, drink of it
Then, if you can!

Still, for all slips of her
One of Eves family-
Wipe those poor lips of hers
Oozing so clammily,

Loop up her tresses
Escaped from the comb,
Her fair auburn tresses;
Whilst wonderment guesses
Where was her home?

Who was her father?
Who was her mother?
Had she a sister?
Had she a brother?
Or was there a dearer one
Still, and a nearer one
Yet, than all other?

Alas! for the rarity
Of Christian charity
Under the sun!
Oh! it was pitiful
Near a whole city full,

Home she had none.

Sisterly, brotherly,
Fatherly, motherly,
Feelings had changed:
Love, by harsh evidence,
Thrown from its eminence,
Seeming estranged.

Take her up tenderly,
Lift her with care;
Fashion'd so slenderly,
Young, and so fair!
Ere her limbs frigidly
Stiffen too rigidly,
Decently,- kindly,-
Smooth and compose them;
And her eyes, close them,
Staring so blindly!

Dreadfully staring
Through muddy impurity,
As when with the daring
Last look of despairing
Fixed on futurity.

Perishing gloomily,
Spurred by contumely,
Cold inhumanity,
Burning insanity,
Into her rest,-
Cross her hands humbly,
As if praying dumbly,
Over her breast!
Owning her weakness,
Her evil behaviour,
And leaving, with meekness,
Her sins to her Saviour!

The vigour of this poem is no less remarkable than its pathos. The versification although carrying the fanciful to the very verge of the fantastic, is nevertheless admirably adapted to the wild insanity which is the thesis of the poem.

Among the minor poems of Lord Byron is one which has never received from the critics the praise which it undoubtedly deserves:-

Though the day of my destiny's over,
  And the star of my fate hath declined
Thy soft heart refused to discover
  The faults which so many could find;
Though thy soul with my grief was acquainted,
  It shrunk not to share it with me,
And the love which my spirit hath painted

It never hath found but in thee.

Then when nature around me is smiling,
  The last smile which answers to mine,
I do not believe it beguiling,
  Because it reminds me of thine,
And when winds are at war with the
ocean,
    As the breasts I believed in with me,
  If their billows excite an emotion,
  It is that they bear me from thee.

Though the rock of my last hope is
shivered,
    And its fragments are sunk in the wave,
  Though I feel that my soul is delivered
    To pain- it shall not be its slave.
  There is many a pang to pursue me:

They may crush, but they shall not contemn-
They may torture, but shall not subdue me-
'Tis of thee that I think- not of them.

Though human, thou didst not deceive me,
Though woman, thou didst not forsake,
Though loved, thou forborest to grieve me,
Though slandered, thou never couldst shake,-
Though trusted, thou didst not disclaim me,
Though parted, it was not to fly,
Though watchful, 'twas not to defame me,
Nor mute, that the world might belie.

Yet I blame not the world, nor despise it,
Nor the war of the many with one-

If my soul was not fitted to prize it,
 'Twas folly not sooner to shun:
And if dearly that error hath cost me,
 And more than I once could foresee,
I have found that whatever it lost me,
 It could not deprive me of thee.

From the wreck of the past, which hath
perished,
 Thus much I at least may recall,
It hath taught me that which I most
cherished
 Deserved to be dearest of all:
In the desert a fountain is springing,
 In the wide waste there still is a tree,
And a bird in the solitude singing,
 Which speaks to my spirit of thee.

Although the rhythm here is one of the most

difficult, the versification could scarcely be improved. No nobler theme ever engaged the pen of poet. It is the soul-elevating idea that no man can consider himself entitled to complain of Fate while in his adversity he still retains the unwavering love of woman.

From Alfred Tennyson, although in perfect sincerity I regard him as the noblest poet that ever lived, I have left myself time to cite only a very brief specimen. I call him, and think him the noblest of poets, not because the impressions he produces are at all times the most profound- not because the poetical excitement which be induces is at all times the most intense- but because it is at all times the most ethereal- in other words, the most elevating and most pure. No poet is so little of the earth, earthy. What I am about to read is from his last long poem, "The Princess":-

Tears, idle tears, I know not what they mean,
Tears from the depth of some divine despair
Rise in the heart, and gather to the eyes,
In looking on the happy Autumn fields,
And thinking of the days that are no more.

Fresh as the first beam glittering on a sail,
That brings our friends up from the underworld,
Sad as the last which reddens over one
That sinks with all we love below the verge;
So sad, so fresh, the days that are no more.

Ah, sad and strange as in dark summer dawns
The earliest pipe of half-awaken'd birds
To dying ears, when unto dying eyes
The casement slowly grows a glimmering square;
So sad, so strange, the days that are no more.

Dear as remember'd kisses after death,
And sweet as those by hopeless fancy feign'd
On lips that are for others; deep as love,
Deep as first love, and wild with all regret,
O Death in Life, the days that are no more.

Thus, although in a very cursory and imperfect

manner, I have endeavoured to convey to you my conception of the Poetic Principle. It has been my purpose to suggest that, while this principle itself is strictly and simply the Human Aspiration for Supernal Beauty, the manifestation of the Principle is always found in an elevating excitement of the soul, quite independent of that passion which is the intoxication of the Heart, or of that truth which is the satisfaction of the Reason. For in regard to passion, alas! its tendency is to degrade rather than to elevate the Soul. Love, on the contrary- Love- the true, the divine Eros- the Uranian as distinguished from the Dionnan Venus- is unquestionably the purest and truest of all poetical themes. And in regard to Truth, if, to be sure, through the attainment of a truth we are led to perceive a harmony where none was apparent before, we experience at once the true poetical effect; but this effect is referable to the harmony alone, and not in the least degree to the truth which merely served to render the harmony manifest.

We shall reach, however, more immediately a distinct conception of what the true Poetry is, by mere reference to a few of the simple elements which induce in the Poet himself the true poetical effect. He recognises the ambrosia which nourishes his soul in the bright orbs that shine in Heaven- in the volutes of the flower- in the clustering of low shrubberies- in the waving of the grain-fields- in the slanting of tall eastern trees- in the blue distance of mountains- in the grouping of clouds- in the twinkling of half-hidden brooks- in the gleaming of silver rivers- in the repose of sequestered lakes- in the star-mirroring depths of lonely wells. He perceives it in the songs of birds- in the harp of Aeolus- in the sighing of the night-wind- in the repining voice of the forest- in the surf that complains to the shore- in the fresh breath of the woods- in the scent of the violet- in the voluptuous perfume of the hyacinth- in the suggestive odour that comes to him at eventide from far-distant undiscovered islands, over dim oceans, illimitable and unexplored. He owns it in all noble thoughts- in all unworldly motives- in all holy impulses- in all chivalrous, generous, and self-sacrificing deeds. He feels it in the beauty of woman- in the grace of her step- in the lustre of her eye- in the melody of her voice- in her soft laughter, in her sigh- in the harmony of the rustling of her robes. He deeply feels it in her winning endearments- in her burning enthusiasms- in her gentle charities- in her meek and devotional endurances- but above all- ah, far above all he kneels to it- he worships it in the faith, in the purity, in the strength, in the altogether divine majesty- of her love.

Let me conclude by- the recitation of yet another brief poem- one very different in character from any that I have before quoted. It is by Motherwell, and is called "The Song of the Cavalier." With our modern and altogether rational ideas of the absurdity and impiety of warfare, we are not precisely in that frame of mind best adapted to sympathize with the sentiments, and thus to appreciate the real excellence of the poem. To do this fully we must identify ourselves in fancy with the soul of the old cavalier:-

Then mounte! then mounte, brave gallants
all,
And don your helmes amaine:
Deathe's couriers, Fame and Honour call
Us to the field againe.
No shrewish teares shall fill your eye
When the sword-hilt's in our hand,-
Heart-whole we'll part, and no whit sighe
For the fayrest of the land;
Let piping swaine, and craven wight,
Thus weepe and puling crye,
Our business is like men to fight,
And hero-like to die!

IT HAS been said that a good critique on a poem may be written by one who is no poet himself. This, according to your idea and mine of poetry, I feel to be false- the less poetical the critic, the less just the critique, and the converse. On this account, and because the world's good opinion as proud of your own. Another than yourself might here observe, "Shakespeare is in possession of the world's good opinion, and yet Shakespeare is the greatest of poets. It appears then that as the world judges correctly, why should you be ashamed of their favourable judgment?" The difficulty lies in the interpretation of the word "judgment" or "opinion." The opinion is the world's, truly, but it may be called theirs as a man would call a book his, having bought it; he did not write the book, but it is his; they did not originate the opinion, but it is theirs. A fool, for example, thinks Shakespeare a great poet- yet the fool has never read Shakespeare. But the fool's neighbor, who is a step higher on the Andes of the mind, whose head (that is to say, his more exalted thought) is too far above the fool to be seen or understood, but whose feet (by which I mean his every-day actions) are sufficiently near to be discerned, and by means of which that superiority is ascertained, which but for them would never have been discovered- this neighbor asserts that Shakespeare is a great poet- the fool believes him, and it is henceforward his opinion. This neighbor's own opinion has, in like manner, been adopted from one above him, and so, ascendingly, to a few gifted individuals who kneel around the summit, beholding, face to face, the master spirit who stands upon the pinnacle....

You are aware of the great barrier in the path of an American writer. He is read, if at all, in preference to the combined and established wit of the world. I say established; for it is with literature as with law or empire- an established name is an estate in tenure, or a throne in possession. Besides, one might suppose that books, like their authors, improve by travel- their having crossed the sea is, with us, so great a distinction. Our antiquaries abandon time for distance; our very fops glance from the binding to the bottom of the title-page, where the mystic characters which spell London, Paris, or Genoa, are precisely so many letters of recommendation.

I mentioned just now a vulgar error as regards criticism. I think the notion that no poet can form a correct estimate of his own writings is another. I remarked before that in proportion to the poetical talent would be the justice of a critique upon poetry. Therefore a bad poet would, I grant, make a false critique, and his self-love would infallibly bias his little judgment in his favour; but a poet, who is indeed a poet, could not, I think, fail of making a just critique; whatever should be deducted on the score of self-love might be replaced on account of his intimate acquaintance with the subject; in short, we have more instances of false criticism than of just where one's own writings are the test, simply because we have more bad poets than good. There are, of course, many objections to what I say: Milton is a great example of the contrary, but his opinion with respect to the Paradise Regained is by no means fairly ascertained. By what trivial circumstances men are often led to assert what they do not really believe! Perhaps an inadvertent world has descended to posterity. But, in fact, the Paradise Regained is little, if at all inferior to the Paradise Lost and is only supposed so to be because men do not like epics, whatever they may say to the contrary, and reading those of Milton in their natural order, are too much wearied with the first to derive any pleasure from the second.

I dare say Milton preferred Comos to either- if so- justly.... As I am speaking of poetry, it will not be amiss to touch slightly upon the most singular heresy in its modern history- the heresy of what is called, very foolishly, the

Lake School. Some years ago I might have been induced, by an occasion like the present, to attempt a formal refutation of their doctrine; at present it would be a work of supererogation. The wise must bow to the wisdom of such men as Coleridge and Southey, but being wise, have laughed at poetical theories so prosaically exemplified.

Aristotle, with singular assurance, has declared poetry the most philosophical of all writings-but it required a Wordsworth to pronounce it the most metaphysical. He seems to think that the end of poetry is, or should be, instruction; yet it is a truism that the end of our existence is happiness; if so, the end of every separate part of our existence, everything connected with our existence, should be happiness. Therefore the end of instruction should be happiness; and

happiness is another name for pleasure,-
therefore the end of instruction should be
pleasure; yet we see the above-mentioned
opinion implies precisely the reverse.
To proceed: ceteris paribus, he who pleases is
of more importance to his fellow-men than he
who instructs, since utility is happiness, and
pleasure is the end already obtained while
instruction is merely the means of obtaining.

I see no reason, then, why our metaphysical
poets should plume themselves so much on the
utility of their works, unless indeed they refer
to instruction with eternity in view; in which
case, sincere respect for their piety would not
allow me to express my contempt for their
judgement; contempt which it would be
difficult to conceal, since their writings are
professedly to be understood by the few, and it

is the many who stand in need of salvation. In such case I should no doubt be tempted to think of the devil in "Melmoth," who labours indefatigably, through three octavo volumes, to accomplish the destruction of one or two souls, while any common devil would have demolished one or two thousand.

Against the subtleties which would make poetry a study- not a passion- it becomes the metaphysician to reason- but the poet to protest. Yet Wordsworth and Coleridge are men in years; the one imbued in contemplating from his childhood, the other a giant in intellect and learning. The diffidence, then, with which I venture to dispute their authority would be overwhelming did I not feel, from the bottom of my heart, that learning has little to do with the imagination- intellect with the passions- or age with poetry.

Trifles, like straws, upon the surface flow;
He who would search for pearls must dive
below,
are lines which have done much mischief. As regards the greater truths, men oftener err by seeking them at the bottom than at the top; Truth lies in the huge abysses where wisdom is sought- not in the palpable palaces where she is found. The ancients were not always right in hiding the goddess in a well; witness the light which Bacon has thrown upon philosophy; witness the principles of our divine faith- that moral mechanism by which the simplicity of a child may overbalance the wisdom of a man.

We see an instance of Coleridge's liability to

err, in his Biographia Literaria- professedly his literary life and opinions, but, in fact, a treatise de omni scibili et quibusdam aliis. He goes wrong by reason of his very profundity, and of his error we have a natural type in the contemplation of a star. He who regards it directly and intensely sees, it is true, the star, but it is the star without a ray- while he who surveys it less inquisitively is conscious of all for which the star is useful to us below- its brilliancy and its beauty.

As to Wordsworth, I have no faith in him. That he had in youth the feelings of a poet I believe- for there are glimpses of extreme delicacy in his writings- (and delicacy is the poet's own kingdom- his El Dorado)- but they have the appearance of a better day recollected; and glimpses, at best, are little evidence of present poetic fire- we know that a few straggling flowers spring up daily in the crevices of the glacier.

He was to blame in wearing away his youth in contemplation with the end of poetizing in his manhood. With the increase of his judgment the light which should make it apparent has faded away. His judgment consequently is too correct. This may not be understood,- but the old Goths of Germany would have understood it, who used to debate matters of importance to their State twice, once when drunk, and once when sober- sober that they might not be deficient in formality- drunk lest they should be destitute of vigour.

The long wordy discussions by which he tries to reason us into admiration of his poetry, speak very little in his favour: they are full of such assertions as this (I have opened one of his volumes at random)- "Of genius the only proof is the act of doing well what is worthy to be done, and what was never done before";- indeed? then it follows that in doing what is unworthy to be done, or what has been done before, no genius can be evinced; yet the picking of pockets is an unworthy act, pockets have been picked time immemorial and Barrington, the pickpocket, in point of genius, would have thought hard of a comparison with William Wordsworth, the poet.

Again- in estimating the merit of certain poems, whether they be Ossian's or M'Pherson's, can surely be of little consequence, yet, in order to prove their worthlessness, Mr. W. has expended many pages in the controversy. Tantaene animis?

Can great minds descend to such absurdity? But worse still: that he may bear down every argument in favour of these poems, he triumphantly drags forward a passage in his abomination with which he expects the reader to sympathise. It is the beginning of the epic poem "Temora." "The blue waves of Ullin roll in light; the green hills are covered with day, trees shake their dusty heads in the breeze." And this- this gorgeous, yet simple imagery, where all is alive and panting with immortality- this, William Wordsworth, the author of "Peter Bell," has selected for his contempt. We shall see what better he, in his own person, has to offer. Imprimis:

And now she's at the pony's tail,
And now she's at the pony's head,
On that side now, and now on this;

And, almost stified with her bliss,
A few sad tears does Betty shed....
She pats the pony, where or when
She knows not... happy Betty Foy!
Oh, Johnny, never mind the doctor!

Secondly:

The dew was falling fast, the- stars began to blink;

I heard a voice: it said- "Drink, pretty creature, drink!"

And, looking o'er the hedge, be- fore me I espied

A snow-white mountain lamb, with a- maiden at its side.

No other sheep was near,- the lamb was all alone,

And by a slender cord was- tether'd to a stone.

Now, we have no doubt this is all true; we will believe it, indeed we will, Mr. W. Is it sympathy for the sheep you wish to excite? I love a sheep from the bottom of my heart.

Wordsworth is reasonable. Even Stamboul, it is said, shall have an end, and the most unlucky blunders must come to a conclusion. Here is an extract from his preface:-

"Those who have been accustomed to the phraseology of modern writers, if they persist in reading this book to a conclusion (impossible!) will, no doubt, have to struggle with feelings of awkwardness; (ha! ha! ha!) they will look round for poetry (ha! ha! ha! ha!), and will be induced to inquire by what species of courtesy these attempts have been permitted to assume that title." Ha! ha! ha! ha! ha!

Yet, let not Mr. W. despair; he has given immortality to a wagon, and the bee Sophocles has transmitted to eternity a sore toe, and dignified a tragedy with a chorus of turkeys.

Of Coleridge, I cannot speak but with reverence. His towering intellect! his gigantic power! He is one more evidence of the fact "que la plupart des sectes ont raison dans une bonne partie de ce qu'elles avancent, mais non pas en ce qu'elles nient." He has imprisoned his own conceptions by the barrier he has erected against those of others. It is lamentable to think that such a mind should be buried in metaphysics, and, like the Nyctanthes, waste its perfume upon the night alone. In reading

that man's poetry, I tremble like one who
stands upon a volcano, conscious from the very
darkness bursting from the crater, of the fire
and the light that are weltering below.

What is Poetry?- Poetry! that Proteus- like idea,
with as many appellations as the nine- titled
Corcyra! Give me, I demanded of a scholar
some time ago, give me a definition of poetry.
"Tres-volontiers"; and he proceeded to his
library, brought me a Dr. Johnson, and
overwhelmed me with a definition. Shade of
the immortal Shakespeare! I imagine to myself
the scowl of your spiritual eye upon the
profanity of the scurrilous Ursa Major. Think
of poetry, dear of all that is airy and fairy-like,
and then of all that is hideous and unwieldy,
think of his huge bulk, the Elephant! and then-
and   then   think   of   the   Tempest-   the

Midsummer   Night's   Dream-   Prospero-
Oberon- and Titania!

A poem, in my opinion, is opposed to a work
of science by having, for its immediate object,
pleasure, not truth; to romance, by having for
its object, an indefinite instead of a definite
pleasure, being a poem only so far as this
object   is   attained;   romance   presenting
perceptible images with definite poetry with
indefinite sensations, to which end music is an
essential, since the comprehension of sweet
sound is our most indefinite conception. Music,
when combined with a pleasurable idea, is
poetry- music, without the idea, is simply
music; the idea, without the music, is prose,
from its very definitiveness.

What was meant by the invective against him
who had no music in his soul?

Doubt, perceive, for the metaphysical poets as poets, the most sovereign contempt. That they have followers proves nothing-

No Indian prince has to his palace
More followers than a thief to the gallows.

MR. EDGAR A. POE lectured again last night on the "Poetic Principle," and concluded his lecture, as before, with his now celebrated poem of the Raven. As the attention of many in this city is now directed to this singular performance, and as Mr. Poe's poems, from which only is it to be obtained in the bookstores, have long been out of print, we furnish our readers, to-day, with the only correct copy ever published — which we are enabled to do by the courtesy of Mr Poe himself.

The "Raven" has taken rank over the whole world of literature, as the very first poem yet produced on the American continent. There is indeed but one other — the "Humble Bee" of Ralph Waldo Emerson, which can be ranked near it. The latter is superior to it, as a work of construction and design, while the former is superior to the latter as a work of pure art. — They hold the same relation the one to the other that a masterpiece of painting holds to a splendid piece of mosaic. But while this poem maintains a rank so high among all persons of catholic and generally cultivated taste, we can conceive the wrath of many who will read it for the first time in the columns of this newspaper. Those who have formed their taste in the Pope and Dryden school, whose earliest poetical acquaintance is Milton, and whose latest Hammond and Cowper — with a small sprinking of Moore and Byron — will not be apt to relish on first sight a poem tinged so deeply with the dyes of the nineteenth century. The poem will make an impression on them which they will not be able to explain — but that will irritate them — Criticism and explanation are useless with such. Criticism cannot reason people into an attachment. In spite of our pleas, such will talk of the gaudiness of Keats and the craziness of Shelley, until they see deep enough into their claims to forget or be ashamed to talk so. Such will angrily pronounce the Raven [[sic]] flat nonsense. Another class will be disgusted therewith, because they can see no purpose, no allegory, no "meaning," as they express it, in the poem. These people — and they constitute the majority of our practical race — are possessed with a false theory. — They hold that every poem and poet should have some moral notion or other, which it is his "mission" to expound. That theory is all false. To build theories, principles, religions, &c., is the business of the argumentative, not of the poetic faculty. The business of poetry is to minister to the sense of the beautiful in human minds. — That sense is a simple element in our nature — simple, not compound; and therefore the art which ministers to it may safely be said to have an ultimate end in so ministering. This the "Raven" does in an eminent degree. It has no allegory in it, no purpose — or a very slight one — but it is a "thing of beauty," and will be a "joy forever," for that and no further reason. In the last stanza is an image of settled despair and despondency, which throws a gleam of meaning and allegory over the entire poem — making it all a personification of that passion — but that stanza is evidently an afterthought, and unconnected with the original poem. The

"Raven" itself is a mere narrative of simple events. A bird which had been taught to speak by some former master, is lost in a stormy night, is attracted by the light of a student's window, flies to it and flutters against it. Then against the door. The student fancies it a visitor, opens the door, and the chance word uttered by the bird suggests to him memories and fancies connected with his own situation and the dead sweetheart or wife. Such is the poem. — The last stanza is an afterthought. The worth of the Raven [[sic]] is not in any "moral," nor is its charm in the construction of its story. Its great and wonderful merits consist in the strange, beautiful and fantastic imagery and colors with which the simple subject is clothed — the grave and supernatural tone with which it rolls on the ear — the extraordinary vividness of the word painting,

— and the powerful but altogether indefinable appeal which is made throughout to the organs of ideality and marvellousness. Added to these is a versification indescribably sweet and wonderfully difficult — winding and convoluted about like the mazes of some complicated overture by Beethoven. To all who have a strong perception, of tune there is a music in it which haunts the ear long after reading. These are great merits, and the Raven [[sic]] is a gem of art. It is stamped with the image of true genius — and genius in its happiest hour. It is one of those things an author never does but once.

THE RAVEN

Once upon a midnight dreary, while I
pondered, weak and weary,
Over many a quaint and curious volume of
forgotten lore —
While I nodded, nearly napping, suddenly
there came a tapping,
As of some one gently rapping, rapping at my
chamber door.
" 'Tis some visiter," I muttered, "tapping at my
chamber door —
Only this and nothing more."

Ah, distinctly I remember it was in the bleak
December;
And each separate dying ember wrought its
ghost upon the floor.
Eagerly I wished the morrow; — vainly I had
sought to borrow
From my books surcease of sorrow — sorrow
for the lost Lenore —
For the rare and radiant maiden whom the
angels name Lenore —
Nameless here for evermore.

And the silken, sad, uncertain rustling of each
purple curtain
Thrilled me — filled me with fantastic terrors
never felt before;
So that now, to still the beating of my heart, I
stood repeating

" 'Tis some visiter entreating entrance at my
chamber door —
Some late visiter entreating entrance at my
chamber door; —
This it is and nothing more."

Presently my soul grew stronger; hesitating
then no longer,
"Sir," said I, "or Madam, truly your
forgiveness I implore;
But the fact is I was napping, and so gently you
came rapping,
And so faintly you came tapping, tapping at
my chamber door,
That I scarce was sure I heard you" — here I
opened wide the door; — —
Darkness there and nothing more.

Deep into that darkness peering, long I stood there wondering, fearing,

Doubting, dreaming dreams no mortal ever dared to dream before;

But the silence was unbroken, and the stillness gave no token,

And the only word there spoken was the whispered word, "Lenore?"

This I whispered, and an echo murmured back the word, "Lenore!" —

Merely this and nothing more.

Back into the chamber turning, all my soul within me burning,

Soon again I heard a tapping somewhat louder than before.

"Surely," said I, "surely that is something at my window lattice;

Let me see, then, what thereat is, and this
mystery explore —
Let my heart be still a moment and this
mystery explore; —
'Tis the wind and nothing more!"

Open here I flung the shutter, when, with
many a flirt and flutter,
In there stepped a stately Raven of the saintly
days of yore;
Not the least obeisance made he; not a minute
stopped or stayed he;
But, with mien of lord or lady, perched above
my chamber door —
Perched upon a bust of Pallas just above my
chamber door —
Perched, and sat, and nothing more. [column
5:]

Then this ebony bird beguiling my sad fancy into smiling,
By the grave and stern decorum of the countenance it wore,
"Though thy crest be shorn and shaven, thou," I said, "art sure no craven,
Ghastly grim and ancient Raven wandering from the Nightly shore —
Tell me what thy lordly name is on the Night's Plutonian shore!"
Quoth the Raven "Nevermore."

Much I marvelled this ungainly fowl to hear discourse so plainly,
Though its answer little meaning — little relevancy bore;
For we cannot help agreeing that no living human being

Ever yet was blessed with seeing bird above
his chamber door —
Bird or beast upon the sculptured bust above
his chamber door,
With such name as "Nevermore."

But the Raven, sitting lonely on the placid bust,
spoke only
That one word, as if his soul in that one word
he did outpour.
Nothing farther then he uttered — not a feather
then he fluttered —
Till I scarcely more than muttered "Other
friends have flown before —
On the morrow he will leave me, as my Hopes
have flown before."
Then the bird said "Nevermore."

Startled at the stillness broken by reply so aptly
spoken,

"Doubtless," said I, "what it utters is its only
stock and store

Caught from some unhappy master whom
unmerciful Disaster

Followed fast and followed faster till his songs
one burden bore —

Till the dirges of his Hope that melancholy
burden bore

Of 'Never — nevermore'."

But the Raven still beguiling my sad fancy into
smiling,

Straight I wheeled a cushioned seat in front of
bird, and bust and door;

Then, upon the velvet sinking, I betook myself
to linking

Fancy unto fancy, thinking what this ominous
bird of yore —
What this grim, ungainly, ghastly, gaunt, and
ominous bird of yore
Meant in croaking "Nevermore."

This I sat engaged in guessing, but no syllable
expressing
To the fowl whose fiery eyes now burned into
my bosom's core;
This and more I sat divining, with my head at
ease reclining
On the cushion's velvet lining that the lamp-
light gloated o'er,
But whose velvet-violet lining with the lamp-
light gloating o'er,
She shall press, ah, nevermore!

Then, methought, the air grew denser,
perfumed from an unseen censer
Swung by seraphim whose foot-falls tinkled on
the tufted floor.
"Wretch," I cried, "thy God hath lent thee —
by these angels he hath sent thee
Respite — respite and nepenthe, from thy
memories of Lenore;
Quaff, oh quaff this kind nepenthe and forget
this lost Lenore!"
Quoth the Raven "Nevermore."

"Prophet!" said I, "thing of evil! — prophet
still, if bird or devil! —
Whether Tempter sent, or whether tempest
tossed thee here ashore,
Desolate yet all undaunted, on this desert land
enchanted —

On this home by Horror haunted — tell me
truly, I implore —
Is there — is there balm in Gilead? — tell me —
tell me, I implore!"
Quoth the Raven "Nevermore."

"Prophet!" said I, "thing of evil! — prophet
still, if bird or devil!
By that Heaven that bends above us — by that
God we both adore —
Tell this soul with sorrow laden if, within the
distant Aidenn,
It shall clasp a sainted maiden whom the
angels name Lenore —
Clasp a rare and radiant maiden whom the
angels name Lenore."
Quoth the Raven "Nevermore."

"Be that word our sign of parting, bird or
fiend!" I shrieked, upstarting —
"Get thee back into the tempest and the Night's
Plutonian shore!
Leave no black plume as a token of that lie thy
soul hath spoken!
Leave my loneliness unbroken! — quit the bust
above my door!
Take thy beak from out my heart, and take thy
form from off my door!"
Quoth the Raven "Nevermore."

And the Raven, never flitting, still is sitting,
still is sitting
On the pallid bust of Pallas just above my
chamber door;
And his eyes have all the seeming of a demon's
that is dreaming,

And the lamp-light o'er him streaming throws
his shadow on the floor;
And my soul from out that shadow that lies
floating on the floor
Shall be lifted — nevermore!

Edgar Alan Poe
(January 19, 1809 – October 7, 1849)
American author, poet, editor,   and literary critic, best known for his tales of mystery and the macabre. Poe was one of the earliest American practitioners of the short story, and is generally considered the inventor of the detective fiction genre and one of the pioneers of science fiction. He was the first well-known American writer to try to earn a living through writing alone, resulting in a financially difficult life and career.

However in January 1845 Poe published his poem, "The Raven", to instant success. He died on October 7, 1849, at age 40, in Baltimore.

James Stettler

Author and film-maker James Stettler wrote his first book - and best seller - at the age of 19. Several Best sellers followed until 2013, when he decided to branch out into documentary film-making and Publishing. He lives in the UK with his wife, two children and numerous animals, both real and stuffed. He is currently working on the documentary – Torso – and several Graphic Novels. He views his two sons as being his best creations.

Lightning Source UK Ltd.
Milton Keynes UK
UKHW02f0630220518
323007UK00012B/699/P

9 781291 948004